Dear Paren

We all lo   ir
imagination   is
to experien   ng
readers, who have learned to   to
sound out words, love good stories. Thanks to the Franklin
Noah Peterson series, parents, teachers, good readers and
struggling readers, all of us, can lose ourselves in Frank's
world of imagination, mystery, the magic of nature, and warm
relationships.

The Frank stories are magnetic, whether they are read in
modified Noah Text or unmodified plain text. For those who
have developed sufficient skill and fluency, they can enjoy the
stories in their standard, unmodified form. For those who
have not, **the stories are an all too rare opportunity to
learn to love to read while learning how to read.**

As children develop beyond their elementary reading abilities,
the challenge is to build on a basic awareness of how **patterns**
of letters stand for sounds, and how those sounds come
together to make one syllable words. Early readers who have
learned these one syllable patterns well are poised to
recognize them as signals for the individual syllables in
longer, multisyllable words. Struggling readers have far more
difficulty. For them, longer words are often a sea of
individual letters. Syllable subdivisions are hard to
discern. The modified Frank books in Noah Text highlight
where the syllable breaks occur so that the struggling reader
can **decode multisyllable words more accurately and more
fluently.**

A key function of those letter **patterns** is to clarify which
vowel sound is needed. The pattern **ig** informs the reader that
a short vowel is needed in a word like rig. The pattern **een**
tells the reader that the vowel would be long in a word like

green. Armed with awareness of these patterns, the reader can more easily recognize and sound out longer words like rigorous or greenhouse.

If a reader does not have well-honed awareness of this kind, **the modified Frank stories in Noah Text will highlight the syllables and signal the long vowel sounds for him or her, never altering the magnetism of the stories.** Here is an example:

Franklin **No**ah **Pe**ter**son** lives in a small New **Eng**land **coast**al town called Port **Jo**nah.

Sarah K. Blodgett, the author of the Franklin Noah Peterson series, watched as her own child longed for interesting, higher level books but was frustrated by those unrecognizable syllables in multisyllable words. She knew she needed to find some books that would highlight the syllables in longer words and would differentiate long vowel sounds, while never compromising the interest level. She didn't find them, so she has written her own.

Now parents, teachers, and our children can learn to read effortlessly while Frank inspires their imagination and invites them to explore the richness of nature and the warmth of close friendships and family.

Miriam Cherkes-Julkowski, Ph.D.
Professor, Educational Psychology, retired
Educational Diagnostician and Consultant

A long vowel is a vowel that pronounces its letter name. Here are some examples you will find in Noah Text:

Long (a)	pl<u>a</u>te, p<u>ai</u>n, **hesi<u>ta</u>te**, **n<u>a</u>**tion
	h<u>ai</u>r, r<u>a</u>re, **p<u>a</u>r**ent, **l<u>i</u>**brar**y**
	p<u>a</u>le, f<u>ai</u>l, **d<u>e</u>**tail
	tr<u>a</u>y, **al**w<u>a</u>ys
Long (e)	f<u>ee</u>t, t<u>ea</u>ch, **com**pl<u>e</u>te
	f<u>ee</u>l, d<u>ea</u>l, **ap**p<u>ea</u>l
	<u>ea</u>r, f<u>ea</u>r, h<u>e</u>re,
	disap**p<u>ea</u>r**, **se**v<u>e</u>re
Long (i)	tr<u>i</u>be, l<u>i</u>ke, n<u>i</u>ght, **h<u>i</u>gh**light
	f<u>i</u>re, **ad**m<u>i</u>re, **r<u>e</u>**quire
	m<u>i</u>le, p<u>i</u>le, **a**wh<u>i</u>le, **rep**t<u>i</u>le

Long (o)	g**l**<u>o</u>be, n<u>o</u>se, **sup**p<u>o</u>se, **re**m<u>o</u>te
	c<u>o</u>ach, wh<u>o</u>le, c<u>o</u>al, g<u>o</u>al, **ap**pr<u>o</u>ach
	m<u>o</u>w, bl<u>o</u>wn, **win**d<u>o</u>w
Long (u)	h<u>u</u>ge, m<u>u</u>le, f<u>u</u>el, **per**f<u>u</u>me, **a**m<u>u</u>se
	h<u>u</u>e, **ar**g<u>u</u>e, **tis**s<u>u</u>e

Note: When the (u) letter is articulated over a long period of time, it creates the (oo) sound as found in the words tube and blue. There are various phonics programs that identify this (oo) sound as a long (u). However, Noah Text does not, as it is only identifying traditional long vowels to emphasize what is logical and systematic to new and struggling readers.

The **Mystical** Years

of

Franklin **No**ah **Pe**ter**son**

Book One:

The **Ear**ly Years

Sarah K. **Blod**gett

Disclaimer: As you will find in the research provided at noahtext.com, the English writing system is extremely complex. Thus, the process of segmenting syllables, identifying rime patterns, and highlighting long vowels, is not only tedious, but quite ambiguous at times based on the pronunciation of various regional dialects, the complexity of English orthography, and other articulatory considerations. In that light, Noah Text strives to be as accurate as possible in developing a clear, concise, modified text that will assist the reader. However, it cannot guarantee 100% universal agreement on pronunciation for all words.

This book is brought to you by Noah Text (patent pending).

ISBN-13: **978-1536848830**
ISBN-10: **1536848832**
Library of Congress Control Number: **2016903689**
CreateSpace Independent Publishing Platform, North Charleston, SC

In **lov**ing **memory**

of

Marie **Yeis**ley **Krae**mer.

Contents

Year Two:
*The **Silver Dollar***

Year One:

The **Glimmering, Golden Spiral**

Staircase

Those who don't **be**lieve in **mag**ic
will **nev**er find it.

—Roald Dahl

Chapter One

A Boy Named Frank

Franklin **No**ah **Pe**ter**son** lives in a small New **Eng**land **coast**al town called Port **Jo**nah. Frank, as he is called by friends and **fam**i**ly**, is twelve years old. He has **wav**y blond hair, big blue eyes, and is of **av**er**age** build for his age. Some would say he's a **lit**tle **quirk**y. He loves **an**imals and all things **na**ture **af**fords. He loves to build **cra**zy **struc**tures in his **back**yard, **es**pe**cial**ly for his **back**yard **chick**ens, to which he has ascribed **various** names. And he loves to draw and read late **in**to the night with his **flash**light tucked **un**der his **cov**ers. **Al**though he may be **consid**ered quirky, he is **ver**y **eas**ygoing and well liked. He has three close friends, whom he has known since **pre**school: **Jar**ed **Dix**on, **Char**lie **Ad**ams, and **Ty**ler **Ja**cobson. **Jar**ed would be **consid**ered his **clos**est, however.

Frank lives with his **par**ents and nine-year-old **sis**ter, Izzy, in a large two-**sto**ry home built in the mid-1800s for a sea **cap**tain named **Je**didiah Smith and his **fam**ily. The house is **ver**y big and **air**y and even has an old widow's watch perched at the top. **Al**though the home is **ver**y old and was once **ver**y dilapidated, Frank's **par**ents, **Emi**ly and **No**ah, **lov**ingly **re**stored it, such that it is **ver**y **com**fortable and cozy. Frank loves **eve**ry**thing** about his house. He knows **eve**ry nook and **cran**ny, and **through**out the years, he has **con**jured up **sev**eral make-**be**lieve worlds that **ex**ist in each and **eve**ry room, **in**clud**ing** the **mys**terious and **mag**ical widow's watch.

On this **par**ticular crisp au tumn day, he **a**wak**ens** to the smell of the most **de**li**cious** **break**fast **fath**omable. This is part of the **Peterson** holi<u>day</u> tra<u>di</u>tion, yo<u>u</u> s<u>ee</u>, as it's n<u>o</u> or<u>di</u>n<u>a</u>r<u>y</u> **morn**ing. It's **Hallow<u>een</u>** **morn**ing, and as far as Frank is **con**cerned, it's the m<u>o</u>st **magical** and fun **holi<u>day</u>** of the y<u>e</u>ar. His **moth**er c<u>a</u>me up with this **tradi**tion some y<u>e</u>ars **ag<u>o</u>**, and it is one of th<u>o</u>se things b<u>o</u>th Frank and **Iz**zy look **for**ward to <u>e</u>ach y<u>e</u>ar — a **de**li**cious**, **spe**cial **break**fast to kick off the d<u>ay</u>.

This **morn**ing, all Frank can smell is a **mix**ture of **ap**ple p<u>ie</u> and **sau**sage. Not **ex**act**ly** sure what his **moth**er is **surpr<u>i</u>sing** them with this y<u>e</u>ar, h<u>e</u> can **<u>on</u>**ly **won**der. H<u>e</u> can't help but l<u>a</u>ze in bed **a**wh<u>i</u>le, **how**ev**er**, **st<u>a</u>r**ing out the **win**d<u>ow</u>, **won**der**ing** what the d<u>ay</u> has in store for him. H<u>e</u> can s<u>ee</u> **a**bove the front porch roof and **on**to their front yard, which is **cov**ered with l<u>ea</u>ves that have **fall**en from their **beau**<u>u</u>tiful, now quite n<u>a</u>ked m<u>a</u>ple tr<u>ee</u>. **L<u>ea</u>n**ing **a**gainst the tr<u>ee</u> is a **scare**cr<u>ow</u> they m<u>a</u>de with a p<u>ai</u>r of <u>o</u>ld j<u>ea</u>ns, a **flan**nel shirt, and a big straw hat. **A**bove that is **Iz**zy and Frank's tr<u>ee</u> house that Frank built with his **fa**ther. On the **l<u>ow</u>**er limbs of the tr<u>ee</u>, Frank and **Iz**zy hung gh<u>o</u>sts m<u>a</u>de of wh<u>i</u>te sh<u>ee</u>ts; h<u>e</u> can s<u>ee</u> them **sw<u>ay</u>**ing **sl<u>igh</u>t**ly with the l<u>i</u>ght **morn**ing br<u>ee</u>ze.

Frank's **bed**room is **ver**y **co**zy. In one **cor**ner, he has a **mul**ti**col**ored kite **hang**ing from the **ceil**ing. He saved up for it last year and bought it this past spring. Frank is quite proud of that kite; the tail wraps **a**long the edge of the whole **ceil**ing of his room. In **an**oth**er cor**ner, he has a **book**case filled with his **coll**ec**tion** of rocks and all things **nat**ural, **a**long with his books and **draw**ing sup**pl**ies. **A**side the **book**case, he has a huge **buck**et of old **Le**gos he's **start**ing to **out**grow but **re**fuses to **ev**er part with. And of course, what makes his room the

8

coziest is his all-time best friend, who **lounges** at the edge of his bed **each night** and is still **hanging around, anxious** to get the **morning started**: **Allie**. **Allie** is their **beautiful** and **gentle chocolate Labrador retriever**, and she **cannot** take it **any longer** as she's **ready** for **break**fast, tail **wagging** like **crazy**. So, Frank **dutifully awakes** from his **semidreamy** state, pulls on a pair of jeans, and slips **into** a T-shirt and **sweat**shirt. The smells **wafting** through the house are **starting** to make his **stomach rumble**, too, and he's **starting** to get **excited** about the day ahead, **beginning**

with the **break**fast feast that
awaits him **be**low.

Chapter Two

A **Morn**ing Feast

As **u**sual, as Frank **tum**bles down the stairs, all he can hear is his **sis**ter **sing**ing **a**way as she plays the **pian**o in the **liv**ing room. **Iz**zy **re**ally does have a **beau**tiful voice and **some**how can play just **a**bout **an**y **in**strument by ear, but it **some**times **an**noys the heck out of Frank — as there is no end! **In**side their house, she is **non**stop with her **mu**sic. **Out**side the house, she's as **qui**et as a church mouse. Of course his

mother would love **Iz**zy to share her **tal**ent with the world. She thinks she's a **mu**si**cal gen**ius, or at least that's what Frank **con**jures in his head. **How**ev**er,** their **moth**er **is**n't just proud of **Iz**zy; she's **ac**tually proud of both her **chil**dren — **ver**y proud. And if they have a **pas**sion for **some**thing, their **moth**er is sure to **nur**ture it. Why else would she agree to **back**yard **chick**ens? It's Frank's **pas**sion, **cer**tain**ly** not hers or Frank's **fa**ther's. Of course she cringed when she thought of the **neigh**bors and what they must have thought when they got them. **Luck**i**ly,** since they've owned the **chick**ens, having **back**yard **chick**ens in a **vil**lage **set**ting has **be**come quite **pop**ular.

As Frank **m**akes his w**ay** through the **liv**ing room, h**e** **no**tices the **Hallow**een **can**dles his **moth**er has put **a**long the **fire**place **man**tle. **A**long**side** the **can**dles are **var**ious gourds Frank and **Iz**zy pl**a**ced there **ear**lier in the w**ee**k. His **moth**er must have s**a**ved the **can**dles for **to**day. **Luck**ily, Frank **no**tices the **home**work h**e** left on the **cof**fee **ta**ble last n**i**ght. H**e** would have been in h**u**ge **trou**ble if h**e** had **for**gotten it **to**day. His **teach**ers and **moth**er are **al**w**ay**s on him for **be**ing s**o** **dis**or**gan**ized, especially his **mother**. She's **cer**tain his gra_des would **im**prove **im**mense**ly** if he_ would just **or**gan**ize** his t_ime and spa_ce **bet**ter, but he_'s **get**ting there. At le_ast he_ **did**n't **for**get his **h_ome**work!

    Fi_nal**ly**, Frank **ar**ri_ves to the m_ost **scrump**tious **break**fast on earth. And he_'s ri_ght; he_ did smell **sau**sage. His **moth**er ma_de them **ma_**ple **sau**sage, and his **fa**ther ma_de them a hu_ge pi_le of **fluff**y **pan**ca_kes. Frank was a **lit**tle off on the **ap**ple pi_e, however. His **moth**er **ac**tua**lly** **pre_**pared sli_ced **Mac**in**tosh** **ap**ples **cov**ered with **cin**na**mon** and **sug**ar

14

and **slow**ly baked them in the oven. It's all **de**li**cious**!

Usual**l**y, they all rush out the door in the **morn**ing. This **morn**ing, **how**ever, they got up **es**pe**cial**ly **ear**ly for the **occa**sion. So, it's nice and **re**laxed at the **ta**ble.

Looking at them all, you can **clear**ly see who **re**sem**bles** whom. Frank's **moth**er has big green eyes and **wav**y blond hair. She's **av**er**age** in height, and her **fea**tures **clear**ly **re**sem**ble** those of her son. As **u**sual, she likes to wear jeans, boots, and **sweat**ers. She's a **typ**ical stay-at-home mom who works part time at a small store in town when she can. Frank's **fa**ther has thick brown h<u>ai</u>r, blue eyes, and is **ver**y tall. As **u**sual, h<u>e</u> is dressed in his **of**fice **at**t<u>i</u>re: a suit and t<u>i</u>e. H<u>e</u>'s an **ex**ec<u>u</u>tive for a **comp**u**ter** com**pa**ny in the town <u>o</u>ver. **Izzy clear**ly has her **fa**ther's **fa**cial **fea**tures. **How**ev**er**, sh<u>e</u> has her mom's big gr<u>ee</u>n eyes and **hap**pens to have long, **wa**vy red h<u>ai</u>r, which **sur**pr<u>i</u>sed **eve**ryone when sh<u>e</u> was born. Sh<u>e</u>'s **al**s<u>o</u> **ver**y tall l<u>i</u>ke her **fa**ther and is **of**ten **mis**tak<u>en</u> for **be**ing much **old**er, which dr<u>i</u>ves her **pa**rents **cra**zy.

"Frank, d<u>o</u>n't **for**get <u>I</u>'m **pick**ing y<u>ou</u> and **Iz**zy up from school **to**d<u>ay</u>. As **u**sual, w<u>e</u>'re going to the **li**brary for Mrs. **French**'s **Hall**oween **st**ory," Frank's **moth**er says. "I know you **prob**ably think it's **ba**byish, so you don't have to go **in**to the **read**ing room with us. If you want, you can just hang out in the **chil**dren's **li**brary. I heard they have a new teen **sec**tion, if that **in**terests you."

Little does his **moth**er know that Frank not **on**ly loves Mrs. **French**'s **Hall**oween **st**ory, but he **al**so loves **eve**ry**thing a**bout that old **read**ing room. He has the **fond**est **mem**o**rie**s of **go**ing there as a young child: the **li**brary housed in that old **Vict**ori**an build**ing, the **read**ing room with

17

its big **circular window** and a large bench built **in**to it, and those large, **vel**vety red **pil**lows. **Al**though he's twelve years old and now in **mid**dle school, Frank can't help but long for those **read**ing room days, but he **re**al**iz**es he needs to be more **ma**ture, so he **de**cides to **fol**low his **moth**er's lead. He'll hang out in the **li**brary. Who knows, he may find it more **en**joy**a**ble, he **con**vinces **him**self.

Chapter Three

Hallow**een** Is in the Air

Luckily, the school day goes by **quick**ly as the kids are **be**ing let out **ear**ly for the big night ahead. Frank **nev**er **en**joys school that much. He feels school is **ver**y **im**per**son**al, cold, and dank, **es**pe**cial**ly **mid**dle school, but on a day like this, the **energy** of the **build**ing is **dif**fer**ent**. **Eve**ryone is **hap**py; it makes the air in the **build**ing seem light. **Teach**ers who are **nor**mal**ly** stern smile, and some **e**ven bring in **spe**cial treats. In **par**ticular,

19

Mrs. **Grab**ner is kn<u>o</u>wn for **hand**ing out her **spe**cial **h<u>o</u>me**made **pump**kin **cook**<u>ie</u>s. To Frank they sound gr<u>o</u>ss. *Who would want to <u>e</u>at a **cook**<u>ie</u> m<u>a</u>de from **pump**kin?* h<u>e</u> **won**ders. But they **ac**tu<u>a</u>lly turn out to b<u>e</u> qu<u>i</u>te **d<u>e</u>**li**cious**.

As his **moth**<u>e</u>r planned, sh<u>e</u>'s **wait**ing for Frank in the **pick**up l<u>i</u>ne at the end of the school d<u>ay</u>. From there they g<u>o</u> to pick up **Iz**zy, and then off to the **l<u>i</u>**br<u>a</u>r**y** they **trav**el. All thr<u>ee</u> of them are in such good **spir**its, s<u>o</u> much s<u>o</u> that they sing all the w<u>a</u>y to the **l<u>i</u>**br<u>a</u>r**y**, and Frank and **Iz**zy d<u>o</u>n't **ar**g<u>ue</u> once.

20

As they **ap**pro͟ach the **build**ing, Frank can fee͟l the **an**ticip͟a**tion** of his warm **chil͟d**hood **mem**o͟**ri͟es** come to li͟fe. The ol͟d **Vic**to͟**ri**an **li͟**brar͟y is qui͟te **invi͟t**ing. As they **en**ter there's a hug͟e **foy**er with a large **wi͟nd**ing **stai͟r**ca͟se. The **up**stai͟rs **hous**es the **re͟ad**ing room and **chil**dren's **li͟**brar͟**y**, so͟ as u͟**sual**, they ma͟ke their wa͟y up the stai͟rs. Of course Mrs. French, the **chil**dren's **li͟**bra͟ri an, is there to gre͟et them first thing. She͟ is the **ni͟c**est and yet mo͟st **mys**te͟**ri**ous **per**son Frank has **ev**er **en**counter**ed**. And for some **re͟a**son she͟ has a **spe**cial **fond**ness for

21

Frank. She **al**ways wants to hear how he's **do**ing and what he's up to. Mrs. French is an **old**er **wom**an. She has long black, **gray**ing hair she wears in a big bun. She **al**ways wears long **flow**ing skirts and tons of **bead**ed **jew**el**ry**, and she **al**ways smells of **in**cense. Frank's **moth**er says she's an old **hip**pie, and she's quite fond of her as well.

Once **every**one is **set**tled in the **read**ing room, Frank heads out to find the new teen **sec**tion. Mrs. French gives him a **lit**tle wink as he leaves the room, and Frank can't help but **chuck**le to **him**self.

Chapter Four

A Mysterious Book

Sure enough, there is a new teen section, and to Frank's surprise, it's in a quiet corner of the library with a little lounge area of its own. Frank isn't really in the mood for reading much. He just wants to sit back in one of the comfortable chairs and think about the night ahead. However, as he starts staring off into space, an unusual, rare-looking book catches his eye on a bookshelf that stands before him. The book is **leath**er bound and **obvi**ous**ly** **ver**y ol̲d. The **ti̲**tle is hard to ma̲ke out as the book is so̲ worn. All he̲ can ma̲ke out is the word "**mag**ical." As he̲ **reach**es for the book and tugs at it **ev**er so̲ **li̲ght**ly, the mo̲st **mag**ical thing oc̲curs. A **glim**mer**ing**, **go̲ld**en **spi̲**ral **st**a̲**ir**ca̲se **ap**pe̲ars **be̲**fore him, **beck**on**ing** him to **tra**verse **down**ward.

As if in a trance, Frank **fol**lo̲ws the **st**a̲**ir**ca̲se **down**ward, and the next thing he̲ kno̲ws, he̲ is **stand**ing **out**si̲de the **li̲**bra̲**ry** in the si̲de yard. He̲ tri̲es to get his **bea̲r**ings as he's **start**ing to fee̲l a **lit**tle

24

lightheaded, so he tries to turn back around. Before him, however, is a closed door with a sign that reads, "Explore the town, your adventure awaits, be back by sundown, you mustn't be late." As Frank is contemplating the meaning, the door disappears before his very eyes. The oddest thing about this whole ordeal is that Frank feels calm, very calm. He is not scared at all.

I'll just go back to the front of the library where I entered the building, he reasons. **How**ever, when he reaches the front of the library, he notices something different about it. It doesn't have the same wide **en**trance he's used to **see**ing, and there's an **old**er cou**p**le **sit**ting out front, **wear**ing old-**fash**ioned **cloth**ing and **drink**ing tea. The **wom**an is **wear**ing a long **ruf**fled dress with a shawl **o**ver her **sh**oulders, her hair in a bun. The man is **wear**ing a **wai**stcoat, a **fun**ny-**look**ing bow tie, and a soft-crowned brown hat on his head. As Frank **ap**proaches them, they look right through him, and when he tries to speak to them, they **ob**viously can't hear him.

When he **en**ters the **build**ing, he knows for sure the old **Vic**torian no longer **hous**es the town **li**brary. In fact, the old

Vict**o**ri**an looks **rath**er new and is, **cer**tain**ly**, **some**one's **pri**vate **res**idence. **A**gain, Frank is **odd**ly not **con**cerned and **re**mains **un**usually calm; he is **al**most **eu**phoric. He has a sense he's **hav**ing a **magical exp**erience and that **eve**ry**thing** will be fine. He just needs to **fol**low the sign's **in**struc**tions**, he **rea**sons: "**Ex**plore the town, your **ad**ven**ture a**waits..." So that is what he'll do....**ex**plore the town.

Chapter Five

Hidden in the Mountain Laurel

As Frank walks to town, the first thing he notices that's different is the roads. Not only are they not paved, there are also no cars. In fact, within moments of traversing the streets, he notices several carriages and buggies being pulled by horses. Again, the people are all dressed in old-fashioned attire. He feels like he's back in the 1800s. And once again, everyone looks right through him; they simply cannot see him. So, Frank **de**c**i**des to sing to see what will **hap**pen, and as **ex**pect**ed**, no one **re**sponds.

"Well," he thinks out loud, "this could get quite **bor**ing if I have no one to talk to all day. There has to be **some**one."

After **walk**ing through town for quite a while, he **fi**nally comes **up**on a group of kids **a**bout his age at the town green **play**ing tag. *Maybe they will see me*, he thinks, but **a**gain, **noth**ing. Frank **re**luc**tant**ly **de**c**i**des to take a **breath**er, sits down at the top of an **em**bank**ment** near a large **clus**ter of **moun**tain **lau**rel, and rests his head on his knees. *This is **start**ing to get **very** **frus**trating*, he thinks, when **sud**den**ly**, a voice **ap**pears out of **no**where.

"Hey, boy, what's wrong? Hel-lo, do you hear me?"

Frank looks up to find a **slight**ly **di**shev**eled** girl **star**ing down at him. She looks **a**bout the same age as him. She has **blond**ish brown hair that she wears up in a **di**shev**eled** bun. She's **wear**ing a nice dress, but she has bits of leaves stuck to her **shoul**ders and a smudge of dirt on her nose. She has big brown eyes and is **ac**tual**ly** kind of **pret**ty, Frank thinks. Frank can't help but look at her in awe. Here, he **could**n't wait to speak to **some**one for a while now, and when **some**one **finally** talks to him, he **be**comes tongue-tied and **does**n't know what to say.

"Hel-lo, do you hear me?" she **re**peats.

"Oh yes, **hel**lo. My name is Frank. What's your name?" Frank is sure he sounds like an **idiot**; he's **sud**denly **be**com**ing** quite self-**con**scious.

"My name is **Abigail** — **Abigail** White. I've **nev**er seen you **a**round here **be**fore. Did you just move here?"

"No. Hmm. I'm just **vis**it**ing**."

"Oh. Well, your **out**fit is **ver**y **un**usual. Where are you from?"

"Hmm. I'm just dressed up for **Hall**oween. I know it's **ear**ly and **eve**ry**thing**. I just can't wait to go out trick-or-**treat**ing **to**night." Frank can't **be**lieve he just said that!

"I've **nev**er heard of such a thing! **Hall**oween? Trick-or-**treat**ing?" **Ab**i**gail** **re**plies.

"Oh, well, hmm. I'm from the **cit**y, New York **Cit**y, and that's a **holi**day we **cele**b**ra**te there. All the kids dress up in **cos**tumes and go door to door, and **eve**ry**one** hands out **can**dy to the kids. I'm dressed like a boy from the **fu**ture."

"That sounds **glorious**! I wish we did that **a**round here! **Eve**ry**one** **a**round here is so **bor**ing. **Ex**cuse me if I look like a mess. I was just **play**ing in my fort **a**mong the **moun**tain **lau**rel. No one is **play**ing with me these days. **Sud**denly, all my friends are too old for such things. Not that they were my friends, **an**y**way**. Who needs them! So, do you need a friend while you're here? **Be**cause I could sure use one," **Ab**i**gail** says in **ex**as**per**ation.

"I'd love to be your friend, at least for the day. I have to be back to my **family** by **sun**down. **Other**w**ise**, I have all **af**ter**noon**."

"**Won**der**ful**! Well, first, I need to clean **my**self up a bit. We need to go to my **un**cle's **gen**eral store down the street. He usually gives me a few **er**rands to run for him each **af**ter**noon** in **ex**change for my aunt's **fa**mous fudge. If she's there and sees me **look**ing **un**lady**like**, she'll have a fit. Then, we can go to the point. There's a **cas**tle there we can play in. Well, a **cas**tle I **cre**ated, shall we say."

"That sounds like fun. I'm in!"

In the **mean**time, Frank can't help but **no**tice how **for**mal **Abi**gail speaks. It makes him **won**der if this is **typ**ical for a girl her age **dur**ing this time **pe**riod — at least if he's in a **dif**ferent time **pe**riod — Frank's **re**ally not sure...

Chapter Six

The **Gen**eral Store

Thus, Frank **finally** finds a friend in this **magical** world he is in, and her name is **Abigail** — **Abigail** White, that is. Once she **straightens herself** up, they run down the street **together** to the general store, **smiling** the whole way. **Suddenly**, **however**, Frank **realizes** he **better** keep a low **profile** as no one can see him and he **doesn't** want **Abigail** to catch on to that fact. At the same time, **however**, he can't **resist going into** the **general** store with her. There is just too much to miss. So, he **de**cides to stay far **e**nough **a**way from **Ab**igail and act **dis**tracted **e**nough so she won't have the **op**portunity to **in**troduce him to her **un**cle. And sure **e**nough, it works. **Ab**igail is too **bus**y **ta**king **in**structions from her **un**cle to pay **an**y at**ten**tion to Frank. In the **mean**time, he's just **soak**ing it all in.

When he first **en**ters the **gen**eral store, Frank can't help but **no**tice the glass jars in front filled with **var**ious old-**fash**ioned **can**dies. There are **lic**orice whips, rock **can**dy, **jel**ly beans, **pep**per**mint** sticks, and **lem**on drops. Of course,

beh**i**nd the front glass c**a**se, is the **fa**mous fudge **Ab**iga**il** **men**tioned. It comes in two **fla**vors: **pea**nut **but**ter and **choc**o**l**ate. H**e** can't get **o**ver the **a**mount of goods this one store sells. It has farm **sup**pl**i**es, h**o**me goods, **cl**o**th**ing, **leath**er goods, **fan**cy **chi**na, and glass. It sells **pick**les, **crack**ers, **sp**i**c**es, and ch**ee**se. There are bins filled with s**o**aps and **med**icines. It has **fab**ric and **sew**ing **no**tions. And in the **mid**dle of it all, stands a **potbelly** st**o**ve, with a **cou**ple of ch**a**irs for the town f**o**lk to sit and talk.

Sudden**ly,** Frank's eyes n**ear**ly fall out of his head when he **re**al**iz**es what he is **look**ing at. Right in front of him, an old man sits **read**ing the news**pa**per, and **be**fore his **ver**y eyes, Frank can see the date on the front page. It says **Oct**o**ber** 31, 1850. He is stunned and **mes**mer**ized** by the whole ex**pe**rience. *The year 1850...how can it be?*

In the **mean**time, **Abi**g**ail** is **fin**ish**ing** up **wrap**ping **var**ious goods in brown **pa**per and string. She stuffs the goods **in**to a small crate and **nudg**es Frank out the door.

"We just have to make this one delivery to the Crandall home, and then we can return to retrieve our fudge. I'm sorry my uncle didn't acknowledge you in the store; he was awfully busy. I actually thought he was being kind of rude, which is not like him at all. There must have been something on his mind as it almost seemed like he was looking right through you. It was very peculiar of him." Abigail continues to ramble on, but Frank isn't fully paying attention. He still can't get over the fact he has traveled back in time to 1850. He figured he had traveled back in time

before **en**ter**ing** the store, but to see it in print just stuns him.

.

Chapter **Sev**en

Castle by the Sea

When they **re**turn to the **gen**eral store, Frank tells **Abigail** to go in **with**out him. **Abi**gail wants to **intro**duce him to her **un**cle, but of course he won't be able to see Frank. Thus, Frank **pre**tends he **does**n't feel well and **con**vinces her he needs the fresh air. When she **re**turns, she has two big **pie**ces of **choc**olate fudge wrapped in **pa**per and a **hand**ful of **lic**orice whips. As **Abi**gail **indi**cates, *it all looks **div**ine.*

They make their way to the point, which Frank is **ver**y familiar with. At the **be**gin**ning** of the point is a large **ar**ea for **pic**nick**ing** with **sev**eral young **ma**ple trees. It looks a lot **dif**fer**ent** to Frank, **how**ev**er**, as all of these trees have since **ma**tured and are **con**sid**ered** the **old**est trees in town. **Be**yond the **pic**nic **ar**ea is an **out**crop**ping** of large rocks, and **be**yond the rocks is a nice **sand**y beach. **Ab**igail leads him to the rocks and points out her **cas**tle to him. Sure **e**nough, he sees a rock **for**ma**tion** that looks like a **tur**ret. Once there, they're **a**ble to block **them**selves from the wind as it's **get**ting **chill**y.

    Throughout the **af**ter**noon**, they **ven**ture out to the **sand**y beach to **col**lect **trea**sures to add to **Ab**ig**ail's exist**ing **trea**sure tr**o**ve, which sh**e** k**ee**ps back at the **cas**tle. **Ab**ig**ail** f**i**nds a **beau**ti**ful** pi**e**ce of s**ea** glass sh**e** calls their crown **jew**el. It is a **blu**ish-gr**ee**n **col**or and fits in the palm of her hand. Frank has to **a**gr**ee** — it is the **per**fect crown **jew**el.

    As it **con**tin**ues** to get **cool**er, they **de**c**i**de to **e**at their fudge and **set**tle **in**to the **cas**tle for the rest of the **af**ter**noon**. There, they **dis**cuss **eve**ry**thing**.

Abigail admits she is constantly picked on by the kids in town. They call her "Oddball Abigail" because she still likes to play imaginary games. As well, she confides that her mother is known as quite the oddball herself, which of course, doesn't help the situation. You can see the sadness all over Abigail's face as she confides in Frank.

Poor Abigail lost her father to a farming accident when she was very young. No one in her family will discuss the details of his death with her as it was too gruesome. However, her mother witnessed the accident

45

and **has**n't been the s<u>a</u>me since. **Every**one tells **Ab**ig<u>ai</u>l how much fun her **moth**er <u>u</u>sed to b<u>e</u> — s<u>o</u> **c<u>a</u>re**fr<u>ee</u> and **lov**ing. Now, sh<u>e</u> **p<u>a</u>c**es all the t<u>i</u>me and is **con**stant**ly** **nerv**ous, **f<u>e</u>ar**ful, and **jump**y. **Un**for**tu**nate**ly,** **Ab**ig<u>ai</u>l **does**n't **r<u>e</u>**mem**ber** her <u>o</u>ld **c<u>a</u>re**fr<u>ee</u> **moth**er and **does**n't kn<u>ow</u> what to do to help her. **Luck**i**ly,** they moved back in town with her **moth**er's **p<u>a</u>r**ents — **gran**ny and **grand**pa, as **Ab**ig<u>ai</u>l calls them. Sh<u>e</u> loves them **ver**y much. **How**ever, **Gran**ny is **al**w<u>a</u>ys **try**ing to m<u>a</u>ke **Ab**ig<u>ai</u>l more **l<u>a</u>dyl<u>i</u>ke** and **nor**mal, but **Grand**pa **un**der**stands** **Ab**ig<u>ai</u>l and smil<u>i</u>es at **every**thing sh<u>e</u> does.

As Frank is **listening** to **Abigail**, a **sudden** **feeling** of **dé**jà vu comes over him. You know, that **feeling** you get when you feel like you've been some place **be**fore or done **some**thing **be**fore but you **re**ally haven't. In this **in**stance, Frank **sudden**ly feels as if he's known **Abigail** his whole life. She has a **haunting** **familia**rity about her he **did**n't **no**tice **un**til now, and it makes no sense at all. And he can't help but feel he's heard these **sto**ries **be**fore, these **sto**ries about her life. It's **re**ally quite odd. But he **de**cides to keep these **feel**ings to himself. As it is, he's in a whole **different century**!

    Before long, Frank finds **himself confiding** in **Abigail** as well. He tells her about his best friend, **Jared**. **According** to Frank, **Jared** is the **smartest** kid he knows, but since they **entered middle** school, he's been **obsessed** with his grades, so much so that he **doesn't** hang out with him **after** school **anymore**. **Jared** is **obsessed** with **going** straight home and **doing** his **homework**, and looks at Frank cross-eyed when Frank gets Cs. He **doesn't understand** why Frank **doesn't** try **harder** in school, and Frank **doesn't understand** why

Jared cares so much about grades, at least at this age.

Frank's two **oth**er **clos**est friends, **Char**lie and **Ty**ler, have new **ob**ses**sions** of their own: they've **be**come **ob**sessed with **play**ing **vid**eo games at **Char**lie's house **eve**ry day **af**ter school, which is fine, "But does it have to be **eve**ry day?" Frank asks with **frus**tration. As he **ex**plains to **Ab**igail, **Ty**ler's **par**ents **re**strict him from **play**ing **an**y **vid**eo games at home, so **Char**lie just eats it up **be**cause his **par**ents are **nev**er home and **could**n't care less. **Char**lie, **al**ways the one **look**ing for **at**tention, loves **hav**ing **Ty**ler over every day after school to play video games and watch TV shows that would shock Tyler's parents to no end. Frank is certain Tyler's parents haven't a clue. There's no way they'd let him hang out at Charlie's every day. ("These, of course, are games they play in the city," Frank stresses to Abigail.)

Frank misses the old days when everyone used to come and play in his backyard. They created forts in the backwoods and paths for their bikes. They even created gnomes and gnome houses throughout the paths and pretended they were at war with them. Now, he goes back there and plays with his **sis**ter. How lame is that? "If **anyone** knew this, it would be **so**cial **su**i**cide**," Frank **ex**plains. But he tells **Abigail** what his **moth**er told him. "She **al**ways says, 'if you look **through**out **his**t**o**ry, the ones with the **great**est **im**agina**tions** — the **odd**balls, so to speak — are the most **suc**cess**ful**, **hap**pi**est** adults.'" **Ab**igail is so glad to hear this and **won**ders if her **Grand**pa thinks this as well as he **cer**tainly is **suc**cess**ful** and has a good **im**agina**tion** of his own.

Once Frank gets **talk**ing, he can't stop. He asks **Abigail** if she **be**lieves in time **trav**el. Of course she's **nev**er heard of such a thing. He tells her **a**bout his **grand**mother, who he **lov**ing**ly** calls **Nan**a. He tells **Abigail** he **some**times **be**lieves **Nan**a **trav**els back in time to her **child**hood. He **fur**ther **ex**plains that his **nan**a and **pap**py come to his house for **din**ner **sev**er**al** times a week as **Nan**a has **Alz**hei**mer's dis**ease and is **strug**gling with the **din**ner hours. Frank **ex**plains to **Abigail** what **Alz**hei**mer's dis**ease is and **re**lates it a **lit**tle bit to what her **moth**er is **go**ing through. **Nan**a **some**times gets **ver**y **anx**ious and **con**fused, and on **oth**er **oc**ca**sions,** she seems to be in **an**oth**er** world. Then there are **oth**er d<u>a</u>ys when sh<u>e</u> can pl<u>a</u>y with him and his **sis**ter and **on**ly gets **m<u>i</u>ld**ly con**f**<u>u</u>sed. **Nan**a, h<u>e</u> **ex**pl<u>ai</u>ns, has a **spe**cial **r<u>e</u>**l<u>a</u>**tion**ship with him, and when they pl<u>a</u>y, sh<u>e</u> **of**ten calls him **Hen**ry. **Hen**ry is **Nan**a's **broth**er, who d<u>ie</u>d in World War Two when sh<u>e</u> was a young **teen**ag**er**. **Ap**p<u>a</u>r**ent**ly, as Frank **ex**pl<u>ai</u>ns, h<u>e</u> looks an **aw**ful lot l<u>i</u>ke **Hen**ry. And when **Nan**a pl<u>a</u>ys with Frank, it's as if, in her m<u>i</u>nd, sh<u>e</u> is back in t<u>i</u>me **play**ing with her **broth**er, **Hen**ry. Frank kn<u>o</u>ws **Alz**he<u>i</u>**mer's dis**<u>e</u>ase **sl<u>ow</u>**ly takes one's **mem<u>o</u>ry** and m<u>i</u>nd and that it's a **horr**i**ble dis**<u>e</u>ase.

However, he can't help but wonder if Nana is just traveling in another dimension on occasion, and on days like this, it seems to make it possible. It certainly makes him feel better to think that way, anyway.

"I've never met anyone like you in my life, Frank. You have the most bizarre ideas, but at the same time, they feel quite reassuring. I do hope there is some peace for my mother in another dimension. It would make me feel a whole lot better too."

Chapter Eight

Saying Good-bye

Sudden**ly**, Frank **re**al**iz**es the time. "Oh no! It's **get**ting late, **Ab**ig**ail**. I'm **go**ing to have to leave soon."

"When will you be back?"

"**Hon**est**ly**, I don't think I'll be **com**ing back, **Ab**ig**ail**. At least, I'm not sure. I just think this is a one-time trip for my **fam**ily."

"Oh, well, can we write? I can give you my **ad**dress."

"Hmm, I'm not good at **writ**ing, and we move **a**round a

lot. So, I don't think so. I'm so **sorry**. I've **truly enjoyed** my day with you. I wish it **would**n't end. And if I could be in touch, I would. I swear on my life, **Abigail**."

"I **understand**," she **replies gloomily**. Then, she perks up. "I have an **idea**. **Follow** me."

They head back to the **picnic area** to the **prettiest maple tree** in the **center** of the lot. **Abigail** hands her sea glass to Frank and tells him to keep it in **memory** of this **special** day. She **explains** that **although** she has **only** known him a few hours, it feels like a **lifetime**, and she will **treasure** this day

always. Then she pulls out a **pocketknife**. (**Ab**igail can't help but **chuck**le to **her**self as she's **cer**tainly the **on**ly girl in town that **car**ries a **pock**et**knife**.) She then carves her **ini**tials on the tree, right on the trunk, and hands the knife to Frank. "I want to carve our place in **his**tory," she says.

Frank, in turn, carves his **initials** **in**to the tree as he **for**mally says his name, "**Frank**lin **No**ah **Pe**ter**son**."

Abigail **gig**gles. And off Frank goes **in**to the **sun**set, **feel**ing **rath**er **for**lorn that the **af**ter**noon** has to end.

"Good-bye, **Franklin** **No**ah **Pe**ter**son**," **Abi**g**ai**l **qui**et**ly** says, with a l**o**ne t**ea**r **stre**am**ing** down her ch**ee**k. "**I** h**o**pe **I** s**ee** you **a**gain **some**d**ay**."

Chapter N_ine

Was It Just a Dr_eam?

Frank runs all the w_ay back to the **li_brary thinking** of **Abig_ail** the wh_ole w_ay. She **cer**tainly m_ade a big **im**pres**sion** on him.

Luckily, the s_ide door of the **li_brary** **r_eap**p_ears as **ex**pect**ed,** and **b_e**fore long, Frank is back in the **li_brary** where **eve**ry**thing** looks **nor**mal. **How**ev**er,** h_e is qu_ite **sur**pr_ised at the t_ime **in**di**cat**ed on the clock. It's as if n_o t_ime had passed since h_e was gone. *How* *could that be?* he **won**ders. Then **a**gain, how could **an**y of this be? Does **an**y of it **re**ally make sense? He sits back down on the **com**fort**a**ble chair to take a **lit**tle nap, but **be**fore **do**ing so, he can't help but **no**tice the **mys**te**ri**ous book is **miss**ing from the **book**shelf. "Huh," he says as he sighs and **scratch**es his head. *I just need some sleep,* he thinks.

    Before long, Frank's **moth**er and **sis**ter **re**trieve Frank from the teen **sec**tion, and they head **to**ward home. On the way home, **how**ever, Frank can't help but ask his **moth**er **a**bout time **trav**el and **wheth**er or not she **be**lieves such a thing **ex**ists. She laughs. "Frank, you do have quite an **imag**ina*tion*." Of course **Iz**zy rolls her eyes at him, which **an**noys Frank to death.

Once home, Frank heads to his **bed**room. He needs time **a**lone to think this through. As he lies in his bed, all he keeps **think**ing of is **Abi**gail and their **mag**ical day. *Was today even real?* he **won**ders. *Maybe I'm going crazy.* And then he **reach**es down **in**to his **pock**et. He can feel his heart **beat**ing a mile a **min**ute as he **touch**es the sea glass and pulls it out for **in**spec**tion**. He **lit**era**lly** screams out loud, "I'm not **cra**zy!" And then he thinks about the point. He has to go to the point. Their **initials** may still be there on one of the old **ma**ple trees!

He runs down the stairs as fast as he can. "Mom, when is Dad **get**ting home?"

"He should be home soon. Why? What's the **mat**ter? You're **act**ing **fun**ny."

"I just know you're in the **mid**dle of **some**thing, and I **re**ally need Dad to take me to the point."

"**O**K, well, why do you need to go to the point now? It's **Hallow**een. You're **u**sually **danc**ing **a**round the house with your **cos**tume on by now."

"I can't **ex**pl**ai**n. It's just **ver**y **im**por**tant** I g**o** there — **ver**y **im**por**tant**! And I n**ee**d to get there **be**fore dark."

Frank's **moth**er is **start**ing to get that **wor**ri**e**d look on her f**a**ce, as Frank is **pac**ing up and down the **hall**w**ay** **out**s**i**de the **kitch**en. Frank's **moth**er is **ver**y **per**cep**tive**, **al**m**o**st in an **un**can**ny** w**ay**. She can **clear**ly s**ee** Frank is **act**ing **un**usual.

Frank's **moth**er is the one **eve**ry**one** g**o**es to for **ad**v**i**ce. She's the one who can get an **in**stant **read**ing on **some**one, **wheth**er they are **be**ing **gen**u**i**ne or not. And you can **lit**er**all**y g**o** to her **a**bout **anything** **with**out

63

feeling judged. So, if she knows something is up and is out of the loop, it drives her crazy.

Frank's father, on the other hand, is the one you go to for action. He'll build anything with the kids, take them on rides, run errands, and you can talk him into going anywhere. He is easy. So, Frank knows he'll take him to the point — he's relying on it. Otherwise, Frank may burst!

Suddenly, Frank hears his father's car pull into the driveway. He runs out immediately and jumps in the passenger's seat before his

father can **e**ven turn off the **en**gine.

"Dad, pl**e**ase, I n**ee**d y**o**u to **quick**ly t**a**ke m**e** to the point, just a quick r**i**de **o**ver there, **be**fore it gets dark. I just **re**al**i**zed I have an **as**sign**ment** due **to**mor**row** on the **o**ld **ma**ple tr**ee**s. I just n**ee**d to t**a**ke a quick look at one of the tr**ee**s, pl**e**ase!"

"**Re**al**ly**? That's odd. You have an **as**sign**ment** on **Hallow**ee**n** n**i**ght..."

"Well, it was **ac**tu**al**ly due **to**d**ay**. I d**o**n't want Mom to kn**o**w. She'll have a fit. But my **teach**er said if I **e**m**a**il it to her **to**n**i**ght — the **ob**ser**va**tion of the tree, that is — she'll consider it on time."

"OK, my son, **buckle** up. We're **go**ing for a ride. But you owe me."

Phew, Frank sighs to **him**self. How he came up with that so **quick**ly, he **did**n't know, but he knew he could count on his dad. Now he just has to **con**vince his dad to wait in the car while he goes out and climbs the tree. By now, those **initials** must be way up high, and he knows **climb**ing those old trees is **for**bid**den** by the town.

Chapter Ten

Engraved in Stone

Luckily, when they drive up to the parking area at the point, Frank's father easily agrees to stay in the car. He needs to make a call for work, which is pretty typical.

As Frank is making his way to the picnic area, all he can think about is being there earlier in the day and how it looked so different in 1850. Once there, he gazes along the lot of trees and is certain he has found the right one; it's exactly in the **area** he remembers. **Luckily,** the old **maple** is still **alive** and **thriving,** and **luckily,** no one is in sight. Frank eyes the tree all the way to the top, takes a deep breath, and starts to climb. When he gets **about** **half**way up, he thinks he sees the **initials** come to view a few feet **ahead,** and sure **enough,** he's right. Once he gets there, he can't help but gaze at and feel the rough **edg**es of the **carv**ing. It **tru**ly is a **miracle.** He must have sat there **stradd**ling the limbs a few **min**utes **be**fore he **re**alizes he best be **get**ting back to the car.

But **be**fore he starts **ven**tur**ing** down, **some**thing **catch**es his eye **a**cross the way that sends **shiv**ers down his spine. It's a stone **me**mo**ri**al and it's **po**si**tioned be**tween the rocks and the **pic**nic **ar**ea. Frank has **nev**er **no**ticed it **be**fore. Etched in the stone, he can see in large **let**ters the name *ABIGAIL WHITE*, and **un**der**neath** her name, he can tell there are **sev**er**al small**er-print words etched **in**to the stone as well. *How can this be?* he **won**ders. This day keeps **get**ting more **mag**i**cal.** Frank can't **con**tain **him**self.

Slowly and **cau**tious**ly,** Frank makes his way down the tree, and ever so slowly, as a sadness comes over him, he works his way to the **memorial**, which says, "**ABIGAIL** WHITE — **Model** of **exemplary service** and **character**. We **dedicate** this park to thee as a place she **cherished** most. She saved **countless widows** and those with **mental illness** through the **many programs** she **established throughout** New **England**. Proud to be one of our own, **Daughter** of Port **Jonah**, 1838 to 1923."

Frank **obviously** knows **Abigail** is no **longer alive**, but to see her year of death in print is **unsettling**. She lived to the age of **eighty-five**, he **ponders**, and she did have a successful and, **hopefully, hap**py life **af**ter all. His **moth**er **cer**tainly was **accurate** when she said the ones with great **imaginations** have the most **suc**cessful lives. Frank can't help but **won**der if what he said to **Ab**igail just **ear**lier that day made a **dif**fer**ence** in her life. She **cer**tainly made a **dif**fer**ence** in his, or at least he thinks she did. Frank's **feel**ings are all over the place. It's like he's **hap**py and sad all at once. And at the same time, he still has this **mag**ical **feel**ing he had when he was with **Ab**ig**ail** **ear**lier. It's as if he can still feel her **pres**ence in the wind.

Chapter Eleven

You Just Need to Believe

Frank **does**n't say much all the way home in the car. His **fa**ther asks if he's **feel**ing OK.

"I'm just tired, Dad. It's been a long day."

"I hear you there, son, but it's **Hallow**een. You must be **exc**ited."

"I guess."

"You are **grow**ing up, Frank."

"I guess I am." And this time, Frank **tru**ly means it. He **lit**erally feels like he's gained years in these last **sev**eral hours.

As they pull **in**to the **drive**way, Frank can see **Nan**a **sit**ting on the **glid**er on the front porch. The carved **pump**kins are **stra**tegically placed **a**long the stairs **wait**ing to be lit. **Iz**zy is dressed up as an **an**gel, **run**ning **a**round the front yard with her friend, **Gra**cie. **Nan**a is **star**ing off **look**ing a bit **con**fused. As soon as Frank **ex**its the car, he makes his way to the **glid**er and sits **a**long**side** her. He rests his head on her **shoul**der while **clutch**ing **Ab**igail's sea glass.

"**Nan**a, do you **be**lieve in time **trav**el?"

"Why, I never thought **a**bout it. Do you?"

"I guess a **lit**tle. I just **won**der if you think **peo**ple can **ac**tual**l**y go back in time and **vis**it **peo**ple from **ear**lier days. I think it would be cool if you could."

Nana looks down at Frank with a **spar**kle in her eye, as she rubs his thick **wav**y hair and as **lu**cid as could be, she says, "Frank, I think you can do **any**thing you put your heart **in**to. **Anything.** And if you want to time **trav**el, I'm sure you can make it **possible**. You just need to **be**lieve."

Then, **suddenly,** Frank thinks about **Abigail's fi**nal words at the point. She said she felt like she knew Frank more than just a few hours, but a **life**time. She said **ex**act**ly** what Frank had been **think**ing **ear**li**er,** but **would**n't say **a**loud. How could they both have that same **feel**ing? Is it **possible** they knew each **oth**er **be**fore? Do they have some deep **con**nec**tion** that **cross**es time? The **sig**nifi**c**ance of the day is **tru**l**y dawn**ing on Frank. Yet, **lit**tle does he **re**al**ize** the **adven**tures that **a**wait him as the years **un**fold.

Little does h<u>e</u> kn<u>o</u>w this is just the **be**gin**ning**...

Frank just n<u>ee</u>ds to **be**li<u>e</u>ve...

Year Two:

The **Sil**ver **Dol**lar

If we could look **in**to each
other's hearts and **un**der**stand**
the unique **chall**eng**es** each of us
faces, I think we would treat
each **oth**er much more **gent**ly,
with more love, **pa**tience,
toler**ance**, and care.

—**Mar**tin J. **Ash**ton

Chapter Twelve

All in a Year

Exactly one year has passed since Frank **be**friend**ed Ab**igail White on that most **mys**te**ri**ous **Hal**low**een** day. It is four in the **morn**ing, and Frank was up **toss**ing and **turn**ing all night, as the clock still glares at him from **a**cross the room, with those **ob**nox**ious**, bright red **num**bers. He has so much on his mind. All he can think **a**bout is the day **a**head of him.

Frank **re**turned to the **li**brary **sev**eral times over the past year **hop**ing to **vis**it **Abi**g**ai**l once more. **How**ev**er,** the **mys**t**e**r**i**ous book **nev**er **re**app**e**ared. And how could h**e** **re**turn to 1850 **with**out it? In his heart h**e** kn**o**ws h**e** will **prob**ably **nev**er s**ee** **Abi**g**ai**l **a**gain, and h**e** f**ee**ls sad **eve**ry t**i**me h**e** thinks of **l**e**av**ing her **stand**ing by the **ma**ple tr**ee** that d**a**y. **To**d**a**y, **how**ev**er,** h**e** plans to **re**turn to the **li**br**a**ry and try **a**gain. He **re**a**sons that **to**d**a**y is **ex**actly one y**e**ar since h**e** took that **mag**ical **ven**ture down the **glim**mering, **g**o**ld**en sp**i**ral st**ai**r**c**ase, and who kn**o**ws, **may**be the **sig**nifi**c**ance of All **Hal**l**o**ws Eve is the k**e**y to its **en**try.

Maybe the old, **mys**t**eri**ous book will **re**ap**pear** on this **ver**y day.

So much has changed for Frank **o**ver the past year, and **al**though Frank wants to see **Ab**ig**ai**l live and in **per**son, he **ac**tual**ly** keeps her up to date on things, at least in his head. You see, like **Ab**i**gai**l, Frank **tru**ly has a **viv**id **im**agina**tion**, and he is not **go**ing to let go of those **won**der**ful mem**o**rie**s of that day he spent with her. So, **imm**e**dia**te**ly fol**l**ow**ing his 1850 **ad**ven**ture**, he takes a fresh, clean **sketch**pad, and starts **draw**ing. For some **rea**son, his most **viv**id **mem**o**rie**s of **Ab**ig**ai**l come to him up in the **wid**ow's watch, so he **literally** spends hours up there **draw**ing **eve**ry **de**tail from that day. And as he does, he finds **him**self **hav**ing **con**ver**sa**tions with her, as if she is with him. He knows this is kind of weird, at least at his age — he is **thir**teen now, you **re**al**i**ze. How**ev**er, he **re**ally **en**joys his time up there, and the **draw**ings he **cre**ates are **ac**tually quite **be**yond what he has **ev**er done **be**fore.

His **moth**er, in **par**tic**u**lar, is blown **away** by his **draw**ings. Of course she's his **moth**er, so who knows how great they **re**ally are. **How**ev**er**, there is one **par**tic**u**lar **draw**ing of **Abi**g**ai**l, where she is **stand**ing **a**long the **sand**y beach **hold**ing her sea glass, that his **moth**er thinks is **mag**nifi**c**ent. She begs and pleads for that **draw**ing, **un**til Frank **fi**nally caves in and gives it to her. The **pic**ture, of course, is now **mat**ted, framed, and **stra**te**gic**ally placed in the **liv**ing room for all to see. And since Frank had **scrib**bled the name **Ab**ig**ai**l in the sand, the **pic**ture is **lov**ing**ly** called "**Ab**ig**ai**l" by Frank's **moth**er. Hence, **Ab**ig**ai**l now lives in the heart of their home.

    Although dull, **sev**enth grade went by **fair**ly **quick**ly for Frank. Soon **af**ter last

Halloween, **Ty**ler was caught **play**ing **vid**eo games at **Char**lie's house. Of course, once he was caught, he was caught! His **moth**er soon **re**al**ized** it was a **dai**ly event, not just a one-time thing. Thus, **Ty**ler was **pret**ty much **re**stricted to his yard for the rest of the school year and banned from **hang**ing out with **Char**lie for a while. **Jar**ed, in turn, **con**tin**ued** ob**sess**ing over his grades, **con**vinced he must make it **in**to some **pres**tig**ious** Ivy League **col**lege to **suc**ceed in life. Of course, to Frank, that seems like a **life**time a**way**. In the **mean**time, **Jar**ed **con**tin**ues** to chew his **fin**ger**nails** down to nothing, and continues to become ever so annoyed with Frank's disorganization and lack of concern for perfect grades. Charlie, on the other hand, is still Charlie. He can't help but get himself into trouble, and he can annoy the heck out of Frank. But he will always be one of Frank's true friends because, beyond the mischief, he really is a nice kid.

Now, the summer was a different story. It was not dull, not even for Jared. All four of them turned thirteen by the end of the school year, and for some reason, their parents granted them a freedom they never had **be**fore. One by one, they were each **al**lowed to ride their bikes **in**to town, and **be**fore long, they were **rid**ing out to the **be**aches. **Luckily**, Port **Jo**nah is deemed a safe **rid**ing zone with **des**ig**nat**ed bike lanes, so it made the **trans**i**tion** easy. As long as they wore their **hel**mets and had their cell phones, they were set. Thus, it was a **sum**mer of **un**a**dul**ter**at**ed fun. They went **swim**ming, **fish**ing, and **boat**ing. They mowed lawns and did odd jobs for **spend**ing **mon**ey to pay for all the junk they **want**ed in town, such as ice cream, **can**dy, fried food, and **piz**za. And their

favor**ite** part of **sum**mer was **play**ing **man**hunt **eve**ry night with a big group of kids that **in**clud**ed** both boys and girls. Yes, girls!

In fact, for the first time, Frank fell in love. Her name is **Sam**an**tha Da**vis. She has long dark hair, **beau**tiful green eyes, and the **nic**est smile. She has a great laugh, a **won**der**ful per**son**ality**, and is quite **pop**ular. **Un**for**tu**nate**ly**, for Frank, she **bare**ly **no**tic**es** him. Like all the girls in his grade, she's in love with **Char**lie, **Char**lie **Ad**ams, Frank's **Char**lie **Ad**ams! Frank can't stand it; it drives him nuts. *Why do all the* *girls have to like* **Char***lie? Why can't one — the one* **I** *like — like me?* Frank **won**ders. And of course, this m_akes **Char**lie more full of **him**self than h_e **al**read_y is. It's a **le**thal **com**b**ina**tion as far as Frank is **con**cerned. Since **pre**school, **Char**li_e can't help but. cause **mis**chief, and h_e's **al**w_ays **got**ten **a**w_ay with it **be**cause h_e kn_ows how to work the **a**dults. *He_'s s_o c_ute,* they would s_ay. It would m_ake Frank want to **vom**it. Now, all the girls are in love with him, which just **bol**sters his **e**g_o, **mak**ing him f_eel **in**vincible. **A**gain, he's still one of Frank's **clos**est friends and **al**w_ays will b_e, but

Frank is **cer**tain **Char**lie is **go**ing to get **him**self **in**to big **trou**ble at the rate he's **go**ing.

Tyler and **Jar**ed don't seem as phased by **Char**lie's big ego, however. In fact, **Ty**ler likes to bask in the glow of it; he's sort of **Char**lie's **shad**ow. Frank would call him a **fol**lower. And **Jar**ed is just **bliss**fully unaware. In fact, **man**y would say **Jar**ed is **so**cially awkward and **bliss**fully unaware of a lot of things. Now that they're all **ma**turing, **Jar**ed's **awk**wardness is **be**coming more **app**arent, **es**pecially to Frank.

At some point, Frank must have **fall**en asleep as **All**ie is

licking and **sniff**ing at his f<u>a</u>ce
feverish**ly** s<u>o</u> h<u>e</u> will **aw<u>a</u>ken**.

"**Al**li<u>e</u>! Yuck! What are yo<u>u</u>
doing? Yo<u>u</u> gr<u>o</u>ss **choc<u>o</u>late** lab!"

Well, Frank is **aw<u>a</u>ke** now.
And did it **ev**er smell good. The
smells **com**ing from the **kitch**en
are **beckon**ing him to get up. And
s<u>o</u>, the **P<u>e</u>ter**son **Hall<u>ow</u>ee</u>n**
tradi**tion** b<u>e</u>gins!

Chapter Thirteen

Travel Preparations

Frank **quick**ly slips on the clothes he laid out the night **be**fore. This time he is **go**ing to be **pre**pared to **trav**el back in time, just in case, **an**y**way**. He puts on a pair of jeans, a pair of brown **leath**er shoes, a plain white shirt, and a plain brown wool **sweat**er. This way, he will be **trav**el**ing in**cogni**to** and won't look so out of place.

As **u**sual, Frank and **Al**lie bound down the stairs and head for the **kitch**en. Frank can't wait to see what his **par**ents have in store. He can hear all of them **laugh**ing in the **kitch**en, **Iz**zy **mo**stly. Frank's **moth**er turned their **cen**ter **is**land **in**to a **break**fast **buf**fet, and it looks **scrump**tious. She made **home**made bread and **blue**berry **muf**fins, and she has an **as**sort**ment** of **fill**ings spread out so they can each **cre**ate their own **om**elet. Frank and **Iz**zy have theirs with ham and cheese, and Frank's **par**ents have the works: ham, cheese, **on**ion, **broc**coli, and **pep**pers.

"Frank, since you and **Iz**zy are **get**ting out of school **earl**y again this year for **Hall**ow**een**, I was **hop**ing you'd go to the **li**brar**y** with us. I **re**al**ize** you're **get**ting **old**er, but it's **Hal**low**een**, and I kn**o**w Mrs. French would love to s**ee** you."

"Oh, Mom, that's not a **prob**lem. I love the **li**brar**y** on **Hal**low**een**. I'll plan to m**ee**t you at the **pick**up l**i**ne."

Little did Frank's **moth**er kn**o**w what Frank was **re**ally up to. Frank **of**ten **won**dered what she'd think if sh**e ac**tua**ll**y knew h**e** had **trav**eled back in t**i**me. Sh**e probably would**n't let him **any**where n**e**ar the **li**brar**y**!

Then Frank's dad ch**i**mes in. "**O**h yeah, and could you pl**ea**se **re**mem**ber** to have your **home**work turned in **to**d<u>a</u>y." Of course h<u>e</u> gives Frank a wink, while his **moth**er gives a look of **dis**m<u>a</u>y from **a**cross the **kitch**en. **Iz**zy just **gig**gles.

Chapter **Four**teen

The **Dread**ed Prank

Frank had ants in his pants all **morn**ing. The school day was **drag**ging, as far as he was **con**cerned. Yes, **eve**ry**one** was in good **spir**its as it was **Hall**oween, but he had **oth**er things on his mind, at least **un**til his last block in Mrs. **Grab**ner's **Eng**lish class, that is. That's when things took a turn.

Every**one** **en**joys Mrs. **Grab**ner's class on **Hall**oween day. It's her day to shine. She

alw<u>a</u>ys we<u>a</u>rs **some**thing **fes**tive, and she **al**w<u>a</u>ys hands out her **home**made **pump**kin **cook**i<u>e</u>s. **Gen**er**al**ly, Mrs. **Grab**ner is kn<u>o</u>wn as an <u>o</u>ld crank — not that sh<u>e</u> is *that* <u>o</u>ld, **how**ev**er**. She is **prob**ably in her **fif**ti<u>e</u>s, but sh<u>e</u> has an <u>o</u>ld, **crank**y w<u>a</u>y **a**bout her. Thus, sh<u>e</u> earned the **nick**n<u>a</u>me Mrs. **CRAB**ner, which is not **ver**y n<u>i</u>ce. There are all sorts of **ru**mors **a**bout her **per**son**al** l<u>i</u>fe that are far from the truth, and of course, none of the **ru**mors are **ver**y k<u>i</u>nd. Mrs. **Grab**ner is qu<u>i</u>te **a**w<u>a</u>re of her **crab**by w<u>a</u>ys, and sh<u>e</u> tr<u>i</u>es to b<u>e</u> more **pa**tient and **hap**py-go-**luck**y. It's just hard for her, but on **Hallow<u>e</u><u>e</u>n** sh<u>e</u> m<u>a</u>kes a **spe**cial **ef**fort for **her**self and the kids.

You s<u>e</u><u>e</u>, Mrs. **Grab**ner **tru**ly does want the best for all her **stu**dents and helps them str<u>i</u>ve to b<u>e</u> their **ver**y best. In fact, sh<u>e</u> has a **par**tic<u>u</u>lar **fond**ness for Frank and **Char**li<u>e</u> as she kn<u>o</u>ws they b<u>o</u>th n<u>ee</u>d a **lit**tle **ex**tra **at**ten**tion**: Frank for his **dis**organ<u>iza</u>tion, and **Char**li<u>e</u> for his **mis**chie**vous**ness. They think sh<u>e</u>'s **b<u>e</u>**ing hard on them, but **lit**tle do they kn<u>o</u>w sh<u>e</u>'s **try**ing to help them.

Well, on this **par**tic<u>u</u>lar block, the last block of the d<u>ay</u>, as her **class**room is **fill**ing up with kids, **Char**lie seems a **lit**tle more ramped up than usual.

"Frank, just wait **un**til you see the prank I'm **go**ing to pull on Mrs. **CRAB**ner. It's **go**ing to be **ep**ic," says **Char**lie. Frank can't help but roll his eyes at **Char**lie. *Here we go again*, he thinks.

As Mrs. **Grab**ner **en**ters the room, she asks Frank and **Char**lie to meet with her **out**side in the **hall**way. Frank is **start**ing to boil over **think**ing they're both in **trou**ble over **Char**lie's so-called prank. *It **fig**ures **Charlie** **some**how gets me **in**volved with this*, Frank thinks. *I swear I'm* *going to kill him, of all days!* **How**ever, once out in the **hall**way, Frank **re**al**iz**es he is **jump**ing to **con**clu**sions**.

"Boys, I was just **won**der**ing** if you could do me a big **fa**vor. Eve**ry** year, I host a **Hallo**w**een par**ty for kids who have **phys**ical dis**a**bili**ti**es and are **un**able to go trick-or-**treat**ing. Well, the **par**ty is **be**ing held in the **caf**e**te**ria this year, and due to our **teach**ers' **meet**ing in the **af**ter**noon**, I can't set up **un**til **af**ter four **o**'clock. **Un**for**tu**nate**ly**, **Har**ry, our **jan**itor, has to leave **ear**ly. As you kn**o**w, I'm **ver**y fond of you both, and it would mean the world to me if you could **quick**ly stop by at four and **con**trib**ute** a half hour of your time to this task. I would **great**ly ap**preci**ate it, and so would the **chil**dren."

As **expect**ed, both **a**gree to help Mrs. **Grab**ner. And of course, Frank is **re**lieved that is all it is. **Char**lie, on the **oth**er hand, looks **ver**y sad and **al**most **a**shamed. They **re**turn to the **class**room, and with a big smile on her face, Mrs. **Grab**ner hands **Char**lie a tray of **cook**ies and hands Frank a stack of **nap**kins to **de**liver to the kids. Right then, you could see **Char**lie's face turn green as Mrs. **Grab**ner goes to sit in her chair. **Unbeknown** to the rest of the class, **Char**lie took a raw egg, **col**ored it with a black **sharp**ie, and **strategically** placed it on Mrs. **Grab**ner's **spe**cial chair with black **cush**ions. **Everyone's** face drops as Mrs. **Grab**ner sits down and lets out a scream. **Need**less to say, it was not the **re**ac**tion** **Char**lie was **go**ing for, and in that split **sec**ond, Frank **pit**ied **Char**lie. He just **could**n't get it right. And poor Mrs. **Grab**ner!

Chapter **Fif**teen

A Whole **Dif**fer**ent E**ra

As Frank's **moth**er pulls up to the **pick**up l**i**ne **la**ter, Frank f**ee**ls as th**o**ugh h**e** could jump out of his skin, h**e** is s**o** **anx**ious to get to the **li**br**a**r**y**. Once **a**gain, **eve**ry**thing a**bout this d**ay** is **ta**king **for**ev**er** in Frank's m**i**nd, and just **think**ing **a**bout the car r**i**de is **kill**ing him.

Final**ly**, when Frank and his **moth**er **ar**r**i**ve at the **li**br**a**r**y**, with **Iz**zy in t**o**w, Frank can't help but b**o**lt **a**head of them. H**e**

swings **o**pen the **li**brary door like a man on a **mis**sion, runs through the **foy**er at top speed, and heads up the stairs. Out of breath, he runs **in**to Mrs. French, who he knows **cer**tain**ly** wants to chat, but **in**stead, to his **sur**prise, gives Frank a **lit**tle nod and a smile, **al**most **sens**ing Frank's **ur**gen**cy**. And there **be**fore him, as he **en**ters the teen **sec**tion, he sees **ex**act**ly** what he is **look**ing for. It's there! It's **ac**tua**l**ly there! The old, **mys**te**ri**ous, **leath**er-bound book is placed in **ex**act**ly** the same spot it was last year. Frank is **bub**bling **o**ver with joy. He gets to see **Ab**iga**i**l!

Thus, he **quick**ly makes his way back to the top of the stairs and waits for his **moth**er and **Iz**zy as **pa**tient**ly** as he can. He walks with them **qui**et**ly in**to the **r**ead**ing** room and gives his mom a kiss good-bye. Yes, **Frank**lin **N**oah **Pe**ter**son** kissed his **moth**er in **pub**lic. She was in awe. **Lit**tle did she know why he kissed her.

As Frank **re**turns to the teen **sec**tion, he takes a quick glance **a**round him to make sure the coast is clear, and in one brief moment, he holds his breath and tugs on the **mys**te**ri**ous book. **Be**fore long, he is **travers**ing his way down the **se**cret, glimmering, golden spiral staircase. He is filled with joy and excitement as he enters the side yard of the library. Once again, he turns around to see the door and sign before him that reads, "Explore the town, your adventure awaits, be back by sundown, you mustn't be late." And once again, the door disappears before his very eyes. It's just so magical, almost dreamlike, he feels.

As he makes his way to the front of the library, Frank is stunned and caught off guard. The entrance of the library looks the same. Then he turns around to look at the street ahead and **no**tic**es** it's p_aved. *Oh no, this can't be_, he thinks, it's **sup**p_osed to be_ 1850. *This must be_ a j_oke.* H_e runs back **in**to the **li**br_ar**y**, up the st_airs, and **no**tic**es** the **chil**dren's **li**br_ar**y** is **to**tal**ly** switched a_round and the t_ee_n **sec**tion is gone. **How**ev_e**r**, the **r_ead**ing room is the s_ame, and there's n_o one in it. And **cer**tain**ly**, the **li**br_arian **sit**ting in front is not Mrs. French! H_e starts to sp_eak to her, but l_ike his last **vis**it down the **st_air**c_ase, sh_e **does**n't s_ee or h_ear him. *Hmm_, h_e thinks, _I'm **ob**vi**ous**ly back in t_ime, just a **diff**er_e**nt** _era **al**togeth_er.* Thus, h_e m_akes his way down to the **sec**tion of the **li**brary where the **mag**azines and **news**papers are placed. Sure enough, it's **cer**tainly not 1850. It is 1995 — **Oct**ober 31, 1995, to be **ex**act. *Wow*, he thinks, *my* **par***ents were* **mar***ried in 1995.* *I'm* **al***most* **cer***tain. Is it* **poss***ible I could run* **in***to them?* But then he **re**mem**bers** his **par**ents **did**n't live **anywhere** near Port **Jo**nah back then and **nei**ther did **any**one in his **fami**ly.

Chapter Sixteen

Which Way to Go?

As Frank makes his way into town, he notices several older-looking cars passing by. One of the cars has a woman in her twenties driving it. She has an old Madonna song blaring on the radio. He laughs to himself when he sees her up close — her hair is huge. It reminds him of the old photos of his mother.

As he walks through town, he decides to sing as he doesn't want to miss anyone who is supposed to see him. And certainly his **sing**ing will draw **some**one's at**ten**tion, es**pecial**ly with his voice, he **chuck**les to **him**self. Like last time, **how**ever, no one is **no**ticing him. Thus, he **con**tin**ues** on and **de**cides to go to the same place he met **Abi**g**ail**. **May**be it has some **spe**cial **mean**ing. But a**gain**, there's **noth**ing.

Final**ly**, as he's **pass**ing the post **of**fice, Frank **no**tices an old man who looks lost and **be**wil**dered**.

"**Ex**cuse me, young man. I can't seem to find my way home. Could you help me get to **Syc**a**more** Street?"

Hmm, Frank **scratch**es his head and thinks. ***Syc****amore* St*reet* is *n**ear* **Ty***ler's house. Boy, this man is w**ay** off track.*

"Well, **cer**tain**ly** <u>I</u>'ll help y<u>ou</u>," Frank **re**pl<u>ie</u>s.

"Thank y<u>ou</u> s<u>o</u> much. By the w<u>a</u>y, my n<u>a</u>me is Mr. **Wil**son."

"My n<u>a</u>me is Frank. <u>I</u> think w<u>e</u> n<u>ee</u>d to head this w<u>a</u>y."

"<u>O</u>h yes, that looks r<u>i</u>ght," Mr. **Wil**son says. "Y<u>ou</u> kn<u>ow</u>, <u>I</u> should have **rid**den my **bi**cy**cle**. <u>I</u> love my **bi**cy**cle**."

"S<u>o</u> do <u>I</u>. <u>I</u> r<u>i</u>de all <u>**o**</u>ver town with my friends."

"That's n<u>i</u>ce. <u>I</u> **al**s<u>o</u> love to <u>i</u>ce sk<u>a</u>te. <u>I</u> <u>i</u>ce sk<u>a</u>te all **win**ter," Mr. **Wil**son says.

Frank can't help but think Mr. **Wil**son is more than lost. He can't **imagine** him ice **skat**ing, or **bik**ing for that **mat**ter; he seems too frail. He's so frail Frank **de**cides to hold **on**to his arm as they walk.

As they head down **Syc**amore Street, Mr. **Wil**son **re**cites his **ad**dress to Frank. He **indicates** he lives at 31 **Syc**amore Street in a **beau**tiful **yel**low home. **How**ever, once they come **up**on 31 **Syc**amore Street, it's not **yel**low at all — it's blue. And it's not **beau**tiful **ei**ther — it looks run down and **di**lapidated. As they near it, they can hear a loud, **roar**ing bark come from **in**side.

Poor Mr. **Wil**son's face turns pale as he **re**al**iz**es he's **mis**taken and **con**fused.

"Oh, young man, I'm so **sor**ry. This is not my home. Do you mind if we sit over there, across the street at that bench? I need to sit down and take a breath."

"Not a **prob**lem. Don't **wor**ry."

"You're **ver**y kind. I can **re**mem**ber be**ing your age once. It goes by so **quick**ly," Mr. **Wil**son says.

As they sit down, Mr. **Wil**son **con**fides to Frank that he's been **hav**ing bouts of **con**fusion, and he just **re**al**iz**ed 31 **Syca**more

Street is his **child**hood home, not the home he **cur**rent**ly** lives in. He **apol**og**iz**es **a**gain, and **in**di**cates** he's **cer**tain he **cur**rent**ly** lives at 25 Pearl Street with his **love**ly wife, June, who must be **wor**ried sick **a**bout him.

"Well, **luck**ily, I know where Pearl Street is as well," Frank says. "I'm sure I can get you back there in no time." Thus, off they go, **slow**ly but **sure**ly.

Chapter Seventeen

A Lovely Home

Twenty-five Pearl Street is situated on a beautiful corner lot. It's a two-story, federal-style home surrounded by gardens and stone walls, and centered in the side yard is a huge gazebo. The home is easily the prettiest on the street.

Sure enough, when they arrive, a lovely old woman answers the door, and she is overjoyed to see her beloved Donald, as she calls him. To Frank's surprise, Mrs. Wilson can **actual**ly s<u>ee</u> him as well, and **imme**di**ate**ly **in**v<u>i</u>tes him in for **cook**i<u>e</u>s and **ap**ple **ci**der. She is so **hap**py sh<u>e</u> gives Frank a big hug as h<u>e</u> **en**ters the house and calls him her **he**r<u>o</u> for **find**ing her **Don**ald. Mrs. **Wil**son **cer**tain**ly** is a sw<u>ee</u>t <u>o</u>ld **la**dy, Frank thinks. Then, Mrs. **Wil**son says sh<u>e</u> n<u>ee</u>ds to **quick**ly call her **neigh**bor, **Li**sa, to let her kn<u>o</u>w **Don**ald is all r<u>i</u>ght. **Ap**p<u>a</u>rently, **Li**sa's **teen**age **chil**dren are out **look**ing for him.

As Mrs. **Wil**son is ending her **tel**e**ph<u>o</u>ne** call with **Li**sa, Frank can h<u>ea</u>r her **laugh**ing and **s<u>ay</u>**ing **some**thing **a**bout **Don**ald not

talking to **him**self at all, and that a n_ice **teen**age boy brought him h_ome. Frank **chuck**les to **him**self. *The kids must have se_en Mr. **Wil**son **talk**ing to m_e,* he thinks. So_, in their eyes, poor Mr. **Wil**son was **talk**ing to thin a_ir.

In the **mea_n**t_ime, Mr. **Wil**son has **fall**en a_sle_ep in his **re_**clin_**er**, as the **telev_i**sion **soft**ly pla_ys in the **liv**ing room. Frank **no_**tices a news **pro_**gram on; **re_**port**ers** are **talk**ing to **Pres**ident Bill **Clin**ton **out**s_ide the Wh_ite House. *Too **fun**ny,* he_ thinks.

Then Frank starts **think**ing of his **nan**a, and how **ea_s**ily she_

116

could have been Mr. **Wil**son **to**day. *What if she was lost in town?* The thought **it**self makes him sick to his **stom**ach. Then Frank comes to a **re**ali**za**tion: **may**be, *this is what it's all* about. **May**be *I'm* **sup**posed *to* **al**ways help **some**one *in some way when I* **trav**el *back in time.* **May**be *there is a* **pur**pose *to all of this.* **Ab**ig**ail** cer**tain**ly **need**ed *a friend to* **con**fide *in, and Mr.* **Wil**son **need**ed **some**one *to lead him home.* He **won**ders if it could be that **sim**ple.

Then, **sud**den**ly**, Mrs. **Wil**son **en**ters the room. "Oh, poor **Don**ald. He must be **ex**haust**ed**. Young man, why don't you come into the **kitch**en with m_e? _I_ just took my **fa**mous **pump**kin **cook**ies out of the **ov**en. They're my **Hall**ow**een** f**a**vorite."

Chapter Eighteen

All about Lily

As Frank **enters** the **kitch**en, he **no**tices the old **app**liances and the hum of the big white **re**frigerator in the **cor**ner, **cov**ered with **pho**tos. The **kitch**en is long and **nar**row like a **gal**ley. The walls are **paint**ed **yel**low, and there's a small **ta**ble off to the side that sits in front of a large bay **win**dow, **sur**rounded with chairs. **Out**side the **win**dow, Frank has a **bet**ter view of the **ga**zebo and **gar**dens and sees **sev**eral bird **fee**ders **hang**ing from small fruit trees.

Mrs. **Wil**son has him sit at the **ta**ble, and she brings over two small plates of **cook**ies and a glass of **ci**der for each of them. She sits down and wants to know all **a**bout Frank. She is so **eas**y to talk to and she **lis**tens **ver**y **in**tent**ly**. Frank tells her all **a**bout his school and his friends and **fam**ily. He **e**ven tells her **a**bout his big **im**agina**t**ion, his **draw**ings, and his **back**yard **chick**ens. She is **de**lighted to hear **eve**ry bit.

Mrs. **Wil**son, then, tells Frank **a**bout her **daugh**ter, **Lil**y. **Lil**y is their **on**ly child, and as

Mrs. **Wil**son put it, she is their "**lit**tle **mir**acle." **Ap**parently, they tried for years to have a child and had **giv**en up all hope. They had planned to **a**dopt, but for some **rea**son, there was a **prob**lem, and it fell through. Then, **mi**raculous**ly**, Mrs. **Wil**son **be**came **preg**nant with **Lil**y at a much **lat**er age than **ex**pect**ed**. She said both **Lil**y and she share a big **im**agination, like Frank. And like Frank, one of their **fa**vorite **plac**es to **vis**it when **Lil**y was **grow**ing up was the **read**ing room at the town **li**brary. In fact, Mrs. **Wil**son **ad**mits she still takes a **gan**der in the **read**ing room **eve**ry time she **vis**its the **li**br**a**r**y**. Frank can't help but **chuck**le to **him**self.

Mrs. **Wil**son **al**s**o** went on to tell Frank that **Lil**y is an **Eng**lish **t**e**ach**er. Mrs. **Wil**son said sh**e** would **nev**er **for**get the d**a**y **Lil**y **pro**nounced her **de**sire to b**e** a **t**e**ach**er — a **mid**dle school **t**e**ach**er, that is. **Lil**y was in **col**lege at the t**i**me, and sh**e** was **do**ing a **re**search **pa**per on the **au**thor C. S. **Lew**is. C. S. **Lew**is is the **au**thor of *The Chronicles of Narnia*, and h**e** was **Lil**y's **f**a**vorite** **child**hood **au**thor. Sh**e** had come **a**cross an **es**s**ay** h**e** had **writ**ten **ent**itl**e**d "On Thr**ee** W**a**ys of **Wri**ting for

Children." There was a quote in it that **af**fect**ed Lil**y **great**ly — so much so she **tran**scribed it **on**to a piece of **parch**ment **pa**per with her **cal**lig**ra**phy pen. It's **hang**ing on the wall near the **ta**ble where they are **sit**ting, and it says, "When I was ten, I read **fair**y tales in **se**cret and would have been **a**shamed if I had been found **do**ing so. Now that I am **fif**ty, I read them **o**pen**ly**. When I **be**came a man I put **a**way **child**ish things, **in**clud**ing** the fear of **child**ish**ness** and the **de**sire to be **ver**y grown up." C. S. **Lew**is. Mrs. **Wil**son laughs and tells Frank it is the quote **Lil**y said she **want**ed to live by. "She wants to **im**part that s_ame love of **imagina_tion** and **fair**y t_ales to **chil**dren, **spe**cifica**lly** to **chil**dren who are of **mid**dle school _age, the ones who are **start**ing to lose their **de_**sire for **healthy**, **imagina_tive** things," says Mrs. **Wil**son with **de_**light.

Well, **Lil**y did **be_**come a **mid**dle school **t_each**er in the town _over, **ac**cord**ing** to Mrs. **Wil**son, and sh_e loves her job. But then Mrs. **Wil**son, all of a **sud**den, **be_**comes **se_rious** and says, "_I'm **ver**y **con**cerned _about **Lil**y." And in a hushed t_one, sh_e says, "**Lily ma_r**rie_d a jerk! If **Don**ald _over**he_ars** m_e, he_'ll have a fit. But I can't help but say it because it's the truth."

"I liked her **hus**band at first, but then they had a **ba**by — a **beau**ti**ful ba**by boy. His name is **Ja**cob," she says **lov**ing**ly**. "**Sad**ly, **Ja**cob has **se**vere **physical disa**bili**ties** and needs a lot of **ex**tra care, but **Lil**y's **hus**band is no help at all. Poor **Lil**y is **be**com**ing ex**haust**ed tak**ing care of **Ja**cob and **jug**gling **eve**ry**thing** else in her life. **Luck**ily, she was **a**ble to cut her hours at work, but I can see she is **ex**haust**ed** all the time. We help as much as we can, but we have our own **physical limita**tions. In fact, we have to sell our house to move **in**to an **as**sist**ed liv**ing **fa**cility **be**cause of Mr. **Wil**son's **wan**der**ing**. We were **hop**ing to l̲eave the house to **Lil**y as sh̲e loves it h̲ere. Sh̲e grew up in this house. But it's not **prac**ti**cal** for a chi̲ld in a **wheel**ch̲air." Frank can s̲ee the **sad**ness in Mrs. **Wil**son's f̲ace as sh̲e st̲ares out at her **gar**dens.

Then, in a more **se**ri**ous** t̲one, Mrs. **Wil**son says, "I̲ **re**al**ize** we o̲nly have a few y̲ears left, and I̲ d̲on't want **Lil**y to f̲e̲el **a**l̲one, her **be**ing our o̲nly chi̲ld. I̲ kn̲ow it mi̲ght sound **cra̲**zy, but I̲ swear, when we̲ di̲e, we̲ will still watch o̲ver **Lil**y and **Ja**cob, and I'm **de**ter**mined** to let her kn<u>ow</u>. I'm **go**ing to send some k<u>i</u>nd of **mes**sage from **be**yond. I'm **go**ing to m<u>a</u>ke it **hap**pen, and I'm **con**vinced I can do it. I h<u>e</u>ar of such **sto**ri<u>e</u>s all the t<u>i</u>me, s<u>o</u> why can't I come **a**cross and do the s<u>a</u>me?" Mrs. **Wil**son's f<u>a</u>ce l<u>i</u>ghts up with **de**ter**mi**n<u>a</u>tion.

"I don't think y<u>ou</u> sound **cra**zy at all. I **be**li<u>e</u>ve y<u>ou</u> can do it," Frank says **re**as**sur**ing**ly**. And h<u>e</u> m<u>ea</u>ns it.

Chapter Nineteen

A Halloween Tradition

Suddenly, Frank notices the time and realizes he needs to get back to the library, so he lets Mrs. Wilson know he must be leaving. "Of course," she says. "You can't leave empty handed." She goes into her cupboard and takes out several bags of Halloween candy. As she empties the bags into a bowl, she hands one of each to Frank: a Snickers, a Milky Way, and a small bag of M&M'S. She then becomes very excited and says,

"Oh, Frank, I have **some**thing else I want to give you. Wait just a few **mi**nutes while I go find it!"

As Mrs. **Wil**son leaves the **kitch**en, Frank stares up at the C. S. **Lew**is quote, and then he **de**cides to look at the **pic**tures on their **re**frig**era**tor. As he makes his way to the **re**frig**era**tor, his mouth just **a**bout falls to the floor when he **re**al**iz**es what he is **look**ing at. There are **sev**er**al pic**tures, all right. And **man**y of them **in**clude a **ver**y young-**look**ing Mrs. **Grab**ner. Yes, Mrs. **Grab**ner! Mrs. **Grab**ner is **Lil**y! Frank can't **be**lieve his eyes. He stands

129

there stunned. **Ap**p<u>a</u>r**ent**ly, sh<u>e</u> n<u>o</u> **long**er works in the town <u>o</u>ver **be**cause sh<u>e</u> is **cl**<u>e</u>**ar**ly the **Eng**lish **t**<u>ea</u>**ch**er at the **mid**dle school in Port J<u>o</u>nah! H<u>e</u> kn<u>o</u>ws that for a fact.

Now that Frank **r**<u>e</u>**al**<u>**iz**</u>es he's been **hang**ing out with Mrs. **Grab**ner's **p**<u>a</u>**r**ents all **af**ter**noon**, h<u>e</u> **sud**den**ly** f<u>ee</u>ls k<u>i</u>nd of **fun**ny, **al**m<u>o</u>st l<u>i</u>ke h<u>e</u> has been **in**v<u>a</u>d**ing** Mrs. **Grab**ner's **pr**<u>i</u>**va**cy. But how was h<u>e</u> to kn<u>o</u>w? Frank is in a d<u>a</u>ze and n<u>ee</u>ds to snap out of it **be**fore Mrs. **Wil**son **r**<u>e</u>turns. H<u>e</u> has to **some**how act **nor**mal. **How**ev**er,** when Mrs. **Wil**son **r**<u>e</u>turns, sh<u>e</u> has Mr. **Wil**son by her s<u>i</u>de, and his gr<u>ay</u> hair is all **di**shev**eled** from his nap. As Frank looks at them both, he feels a lot **bet**ter. They are such nice **peo**ple; their **pres**ence in the **kitch**en makes him feel **bet**ter im**me**diate**ly**. He **should**n't feel bad, he **re**al**iz**es. They **cer**tain**ly would**n't mind if they knew he was **ac**tua**lly** Mrs. **Grab**ner's **stu**dent from the **fu**ture. Or, at least, he thinks…

Sudden**ly**, with a big smile, Mr. **Wil**son hands Frank a **sil**ver **dol**lar. "**Be**cause you're such a kind boy, we want you to be part of our **spe**cial **Hallo**w**een** **tra**di**tion**. You see, **ev**er since our **Lil**y was young, I've **giv**en her a **sil**ver **dol**lar for

Halloween. And now, I do the same for our **grand**son, **Ja**cob. This year, I want you to have one as well. Make sure you put it some place safe **be**cause it could be worth **some**thing **some**day. You **nev**er know! And thank you for **bring**ing me home to my June."

They then walk Frank to the door. Mrs. **Wil**son gives Frank a big hug and can't **re**sist but kiss his cheek while Mr. **Wil**son shakes his hand good-bye.

Chapter **Twen**ty

More **A**like Than **Dif**ferent

Before long, Frank is back in the teen **sec**tion of the **li**brary, and like last time, time has **pret**ty much stood still while he was gone. He still can't get over the fact he spent the **af**ter**noon** with Mrs. **Grab**ner's **par**ents of all **peo**ple. Frank sits there and **pon**ders it for a while. Soon, **how**ever, his **moth**er and **sis**ter are **leav**ing the **read**ing room with the rest of the kids and **par**ents. Mrs. French comes over to see how

Frank is **do**ing. And **be**fore long, they are **head**ing home.

On the way home, Frank can't help but ask his **moth**er when she and his dad had **mar**ried, and sure **e**nough, it was 1995. Frank laughs to **him**self.

When they **ar**rive home, Frank runs up to his **bed**room. He is **ex**haust**ed** and needs to sort through his **re**cent **adven**ture a **lit**tle more in his head. He takes the **can**dy out of his **pock**ets **a**long with the **sil**ver **dol**lar. He **plac**es the **can**dy on his **bu**reau and lays in bed **star**ing out the **win**dow, **sil**ver **dol**lar in hand, **think**ing **a**bout poor Mrs. **Grab**ner. Frank keeps

thinking of the **pic**tures of her on the **re**frig**era**tor. She looked so young and **care**free. Frank can't get **o**ver the **i**de**as** she had in **col**lege. *Mrs. Grab**ner want**ed to teach **mid**dle school to **pre**serve our **im**agina**tions.** How cool is that?* Frank **nev**er would have thought that, but then he starts to think of some of the things she's shared with them **through**out her **class**es. It dawns on him that he **does**n't pay **at**ten**tion** the way he should. *Who would have thought she is **sim**ilar to me…?*

Then Frank thinks about Mrs. **Wil**son and her **con**vic**tion** of **send**ing Mrs. **Grab**ner a **mes**sage once she's gone to let Mrs. **Grab**ner know she's not **a**lone. Then he **sud**denly **re**aliz**es** she is gone — 1995 was quite a long time **a**go. By now, they both **cer**tainly have died. Then he **won**ders how Mrs. **Grab**ner is **do**ing with her child and jerk of a **hus**band. By now, her son must be grown. **May**be things **have**n't gone so well for her. **May**be that's why she's **al**ways so **crab**by.

Suddenly, he **re**mem**bers** he's **sup**posed to help Mrs. **Grab**ner **to**day at four **o**'clock. Then it hits him; he **re**aliz**es** what he needs to do. He bolts off his bed and runs **down**stairs.

"Mom, I **for**got to tell you. I need to go back to school to help Mrs. **Grab**ner set up for a **Hall**ow**een par**ty she's **hav**ing in the **caf**et**e**ria. Do you mind if I ride my bike there? I should **eas**ily be home by five."

"**O**K, Frank, but if you're **run**ning late for **an**y **rea**son, call me, and I'll come pick you up and throw your bike in the back of my car. I don't want you **rid**ing home in the dark."

"I **prom**ise."

Chapter Twenty-One

Life Is Truly Magical

Frank **decides** to get to the **middle** school **early**, **before** Charlie **arrives**. Once in the **building**, Frank can hear all the **teachers** in the **cafeteria**, so he **decides** to wait for Mrs. **Grabner** in her **classroom**. Frank sits there quite a while when, **suddenly**, he hears all the **teachers disperse**. Then, **before** long, Mrs. **Grabner enters** her **classroom** and is quite **surprised** to see Frank **waiting** for her.

"Why, Frank, you're here early. I have a few things I need to do before we get started."

"Well, actually, I came here early to talk to you," says Frank.

"Oh, OK." Mrs. Grabner sits down at a desk beside Frank.

"Well, you know that house on Pearl Street? The one on the corner, with the stone walls and the gazebo," Frank gently says.

Mrs. Grabner's eyes widen and she looks a little flushed. "Yes, I do, Frank. Why do you ask?"

"Well, I was walking by that house earlier today, and as I

was **walk**ing **a**long, I **spot**ted a piece of **glim**mer**ing silver** from the **cor**ner of my eye. It came from the stone wall; it was a **silver dol**lar. It was **some**how lodged **be**tween the rocks."

Mrs. **Grab**ner can feel her heart in her **stom**ach. She can't **be**lieve what Frank is **say**ing. She is **flab**ber**gast**ed.

"**Any**way," Frank **contin**ues, "for some **rea**son, I have this strong **feel**ing I'm **sup**posed to give it to you. I don't know why, but I just know I am."

As he hands Mrs. **Grab**ner the **silver dol**lar, tears of joy run down her face. **Sud**den**ly**, she has so much love and joy in her heart she feels as though she can burst.

"Frank, you don't know how much this means to me. It's a **miracle** of a **life**time." Then she goes on to **ex**plain her **fam**ily **tra**dition and how she grew up in that **ver**y home. She **men**tions how her **moth**er swore she would send her a sign that her **par**ents were **watch**ing over her when they were gone, and sure enough, this must be the sign. Her **fa**ther died **man**y years **a**go, but her **moth**er died a **lit**tle over a year **a**go. She lived much **long**er than they **ev**er **ex**pected and was **fair**ly **health**y up to the end. Mrs. Grabner's face is **glow**ing as she speaks, and she **ap**pears much **soft**er. She looks more like the **per**son Frank had seen in the **pic**tures on the **re**frig**era**tor **ear**lier that day.

"You know, Frank, my **par**ents would have loved you. Just like you they were **pas**sion**ate** about **na**ture. They **plant**ed **gar**dens and fruit trees **through**out our yard. It was a **won**der**ful** place to grow up; they made it feel so **mag**i**cal**. They had a true **ap**pre**cia**tion for the **nat**u**ral** world and loved to share that **ap**pre**cia**tion with others. By **any** chance, are you **fa**mil**iar** with the **his**tor**ic ma**ple trees at the point?"

"Sure, I am," Frank says with a **lit**tle **hesita**tion in his voice.

"Well, when I was **lit**tle the town **want**ed to cut them down to **en**large the **park**ing lot **lo**c**a**t**ed** there. My **par**ents were **out**r**a**ged. The **ma**ple tr**ee**s were **plant**ed in the 1800s but were still **ver**y **healthy**. They **could**n't **im**agine the point **with**out them; they felt they **be**longed there. My **par**ents wrote **let**ters **a**bout it to the **may**or, the **lo**cal **news**p**a**per, and to **an**y**one** who would **lis**ten. Of course I thought they were **cra**zy at the t**i**me. Well, as you can see the tr**ee**s were s**a**ved and they're still **thriv**ing. And I must say, **eve**ry time I go to the point I'm in awe of those trees. Oh, the **sto**ries they could tell if **on**ly they could speak. And I'm **als**o **re**minded of how **luck**y I am to have had such **wonder**ful **par**ents. They weren't **cra**zy at all **a**bout **sav**ing those trees. I was just too young to see it."

Once **a**gain, Frank is in a daze **up**on **mak**ing **an**oth**er** **mys**tical **dis**cov**er**y. The **Wil**sons not **on**ly saved those old **ma**ples, they saved the one **spe**cial tree he shared with **Abi**g**ail**, the tree he climbed to **con**firm her **ex**ist**ence**. *Could it be a coincidence?* he **won**ders — *no, it* *can't be! There has to be a connection.* Frank is **truly realiz**ing the **magni**tude of this world and **be**comes **ex**cited **think**ing of all the **dis**cover**ies** that lay **a**head — the **mys**ti**cal dis**cover**ies**, that is.

Then, **sud**den**ly**, Mrs. **Grab**ner **realiz**es the time and asks Frank to give her a **lit**tle time **al**one to get **her**self **to**gethe**r be**fore they set up for the **par**ty. She feels she needs to **col**lect her thoughts and clear her head a bit.

As Frank is **leav**ing the room, he's **feel**ing overwhelmed **him**self. Like Mrs. **Grab**ner, he's filled with pure joy and elation. But he **also** has a **cer**tainty about **him**self he didn't have **be**fore. He's **be**come **cer**tain this is why he was sent back in time — to **ca**rry out Mrs. **Wil**son's **mis**sion, to send her **daugh**ter a **mes**sage from **be**yond, and to let Mrs. **Grab**ner know she is **be**ing watched over and **eve**ry**thing** is all right.

Then, **sud**den**ly**, Mrs. **Grab**ner stops Frank and says, "Frank, you **re**al**ize**...life is **tru**ly **mag**ical, don't you?"

"Yes, I do, Mrs. **Grab**ner. Yes, I do."

About the Author:

Sarah K. Blodgett is the author of *The Mystical Years of Franklin Noah Peterson* book series and *Zack* early readers. She is the mother of two children, who she raised with her husband, David, among lots of animals, nature, music, and art. And yes, they do have backyard chickens! Sarah is also the developer of Noah Text, a specialized text designed to assist and teach new and struggling readers to read with fluency and ease. Her current book series is available in plain text or in Noah Text.

Over the years, Sarah has compiled research showing that the English writing system is one of the most unpredictable writing systems in the world requiring two to three times more reading instruction time and practice. The research she compiled also shows that English readers often self-correct while reading. In other words, our irregular, crazy writing system trips us up! Thus, Sarah decided to make our writing system more predictable by simulating what predictable languages have that we don't — visibly clear and consistent patterns! She's done this by highlighting critical patterns within words. The research behind this technique is clear. As humans, we learn the world around us through patterns. Noah Text is simply giving readers the key to the puzzle!

For more information and access to her books, please go to www.noahtext.com.